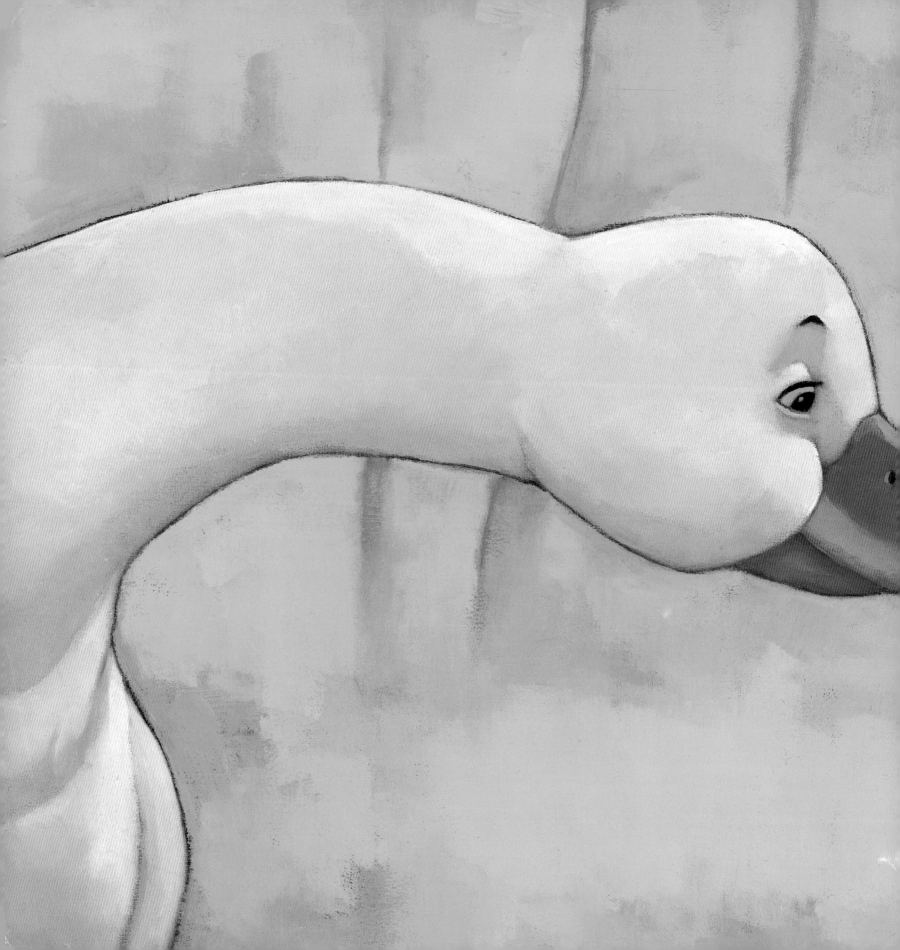

But even Mama's littlest duckling was not so little anymore.
"It's time to leave the nest," she said one day.

"Come, little ducklings," Mama called.
"Paddle on the water with me."
The five little ducklings squeezed close in the nest.
"No, Mama, no!" they cried. "We're too scared!"
"You can do it," Mama said. "I know you can."

Count along with the
Quack – u – lator!

No ducklings in the pond

All at once, Widdle felt very brave.
She jumped into the pond –

SPLISH!

"Look!" she cried. "Look at me!"

Now four little ducklings snuggled close in the nest.
"Come, little ducklings," Mama called again.
"Paddle on the water with me."
"No, Mama, no! We're too scared!" cried Waddle,
Piddle, Puddle, and Little Quack.
"You can do it," Mama said. "I know you can."

🦆 = 1

One duckling in the pond

Then Waddle felt very brave.
He plopped into the pond –
SPLASH!

"Hooray!" he cried. "Hooray for me!"

Now three little ducklings clung close in the nest.
"Come, little ducklings," Mama called again.
"Paddle on the water with me."
"No, Mama, no! We're too scared!" cried Piddle,
Puddle, and Little Quack.
"You can do it," Mama said. "I know you can."

🦆 + 🦆 = 2

Two ducklings in the pond

Then Piddle, for a moment, felt very brave.
She wiggled into the water –

SPLOOSH!

"It's fun!" she cried. "It's lots of fun!"

Now two little ducklings cuddled close in the nest.
"Come, little ducklings," Mama called again.
"Paddle on the water with me."
"No, Mama, no! We're too scared!" cried Puddle
and Little Quack.
"You can do it," Mama said. "I know you can."

Three ducklings in the pond

At last, Puddle felt very brave too.
He leapt into the water –

SPLOSH!

"Wait!" he cried. "Wait for me!"

That left just one little duckling in the nest –
just one Little Quack.

$$🦆 + 🦆 + 🦆 + 🦆 = 4$$

"Come, little duckling!" Mama called once more.
"Paddle on the water with me."
"No, Mama, no!" cried Little Quack. "I'm
scared! I'm just too scared!"
"You can do it," Mama said.
"We know you can!" said Widdle, Waddle,
Piddle, and Puddle.

Four ducklings in the pond

Little Quack looked at the water.
He sniffed the water.
He touched the water with his foot.
Could he do it? Did he dare?

SPLOSH!

– into the water he plunged.
"I did it!" he cried. "I really did it!"
"I always knew you could," Mama said.

Then off they went, five little ducklings proud as can be – Widdle, Waddle, Piddle, Puddle, and brave Little Quack.

🦆 + 🦆 + 🦆 + 🦆 + 🦆 = 5

Five ducklings in the pond

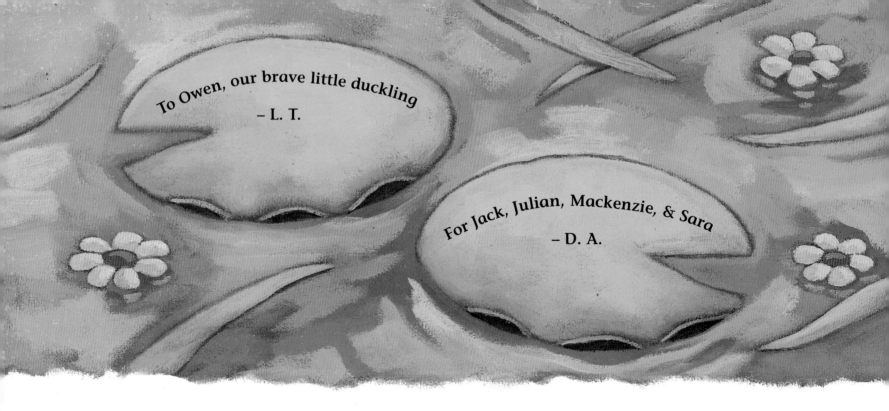

To Owen, our brave little duckling
– L. T.

For Jack, Julian, Mackenzie, & Sara
– D. A.

POCKET
BOOKS

First published in Great Britain in 2003 by Simon & Schuster UK Ltd
Africa House, 64-78 Kingsway, London WC2B 6AH

Originally published in 2003 by Simon & Schuster Books for Young Readers
an imprint of Simon & Schuster Children's Publishing Division, New York

This edition published in 2004 by Pocket Books,
an imprint of Simon & Schuster UK Ltd

Text copyright © 2003 by Lauren Thompson
Illustrations copyright © 2003 by Derek Anderson

The rights of Lauren Thompson and Derek Anderson to be identified as the author and illustrator of
this work have been asserted by them in accordance with the Copyright, Designs and Patents Act, 1988

Book design by Greg Stadnyk.
The text for this book is set in Stone Informal
The illustrations for this book are rendered in acrylic on canvas.

A CIP catalogue record for this book is available from the British Library upon request

ISBN 0 743 47834 7

Printed in China

1 3 5 7 9 10 8 6 4 2